You Are My Favorite Color

Written by Gillian Sze

Illustrated by Nina Mata

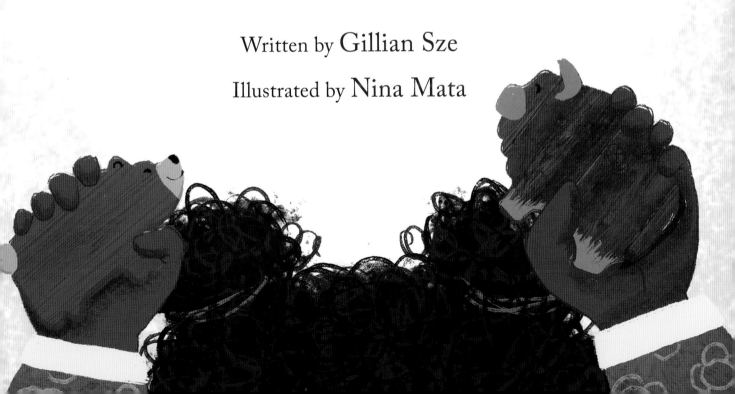

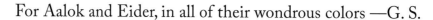

For Aalok and Eider, in all of their wondrous colors —G. S.

To my beautiful Aria Rose, whose face always
lights up my whole world —N. M.

PHILOMEL BOOKS
An imprint of Penguin Random House LLC, New York

First published in the United States of America by Philomel Books,
an imprint of Penguin Random House LLC, 2022

Text copyright © 2022 by Gillian Sze
Illustrations copyright © 2022 by Nina Mata

Visit us online at penguinrandomhouse.com.

Library of Congress Cataloging-in-Publication Data is available.

Manufactured in China

ISBN 9780593203101

1 3 5 7 9 10 8 6 4 2

TOPL

Edited by Talia Benamy
Design by Monique Sterling
Text set in Adobe Caslon

Artwork created with Photoshop CC 2021 and good vibes.

When you ask me why your skin is brown,
I will tell you that you are my favorite color.

I will say that your skin was decided long, long ago. Time was just waiting for you.

I will tell you that you share your
color with the mightiest animals . . .

The brawny bear
whose paws know the
ground of its home,

and the powerful ox
that stands immovable
and at peace.

I will tell you that you possess the gentleness of animals the same hue. You are the new fawn blinking at sunlight.

You are the sparrow, flying through
the world as the herald of spring.

When you ask me why your skin is brown, I will compare you to the sweetness of dates, and to the perfection of the bottoms of freshly baked cookies.

I will gather you in my arms
and say that when I look *really*,
really closely at you,

I can spy warm flecks of precious gold.

I will invite you to listen to the wild cattails whispering in the wind, and to the cello with its notes deep and clear.

Whether you are as quiet as a bud or taking center stage,

everything has its sound, I will say,

so whoop, sing, ask questions, and tell your story.

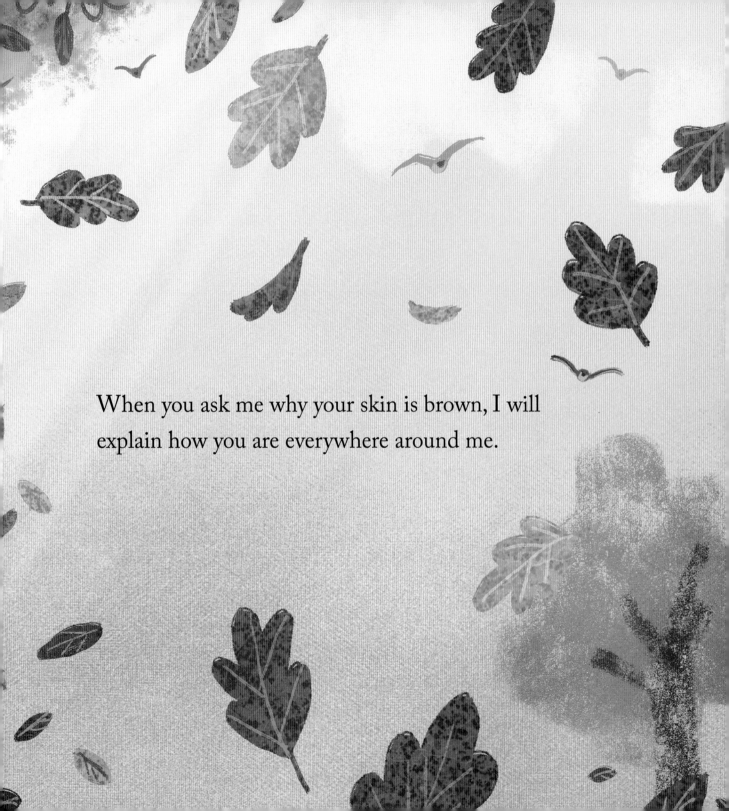

When you ask me why your skin is brown, I will explain how you are everywhere around me.

I see you in the sandy shore
that the sea rushes to greet,

and in the sequoia tree that
reaches up and touches the sun.

I recognize you in the glossy
shells of roasted chestnuts,

and in the butterfly that rests, calm and thoughtful.

I will tell you that your color
found its canvas on only you.

When you ask me why your skin is brown,
I will remind you that hickory is strong.

I will teach you that we
have always built with clay.

I will tell you how you have shades of color
that only you can discover and express.

When you ask me why your skin is brown,
I will say it was magic that waited for you.

And I will promise, always, that you are my favorite color.